To Rod, Happy Christmas!

DENHOLME SCRIBES SCRIBBLING AGAIN

SOME MORE OF OUR STORIES

DECEMBER 2023

DENHOLME SCRIBES.

Love Julie xx

COPYRIGHT

Copyright © 2023 by Denholme Scribes
All rights reserved.
No part of this book may be reproduced in any form or by any electronic or mechanical means, including information storage and retrieval systems, without written permission from the author, except for the use of brief quotations in a book review.

Cover Art by http://www.fiverr.com/designrans
Cover Illustration by Kathryn M. Holgate

FAST FOOD BY MATTHEW HOLGATE

A baker's apprentice is working. He's tired of making crusty round loaves and would like to experiment to make different kinds of bread, but the owner of the bakery feels that the people of Paris want the classic white cottage style of bread.

Mr. Debois only had a small blob of dough and it wasn't enough for a regular, round, crusty loaf. Albert was thinking it was a shame to waste the dough, so he began to shape it into a long thin rocket shape.

Once the baguette had baked and cooled Albert hid it, hoping Mr. Debois wouldn't find it in his locker underneath the running vest and trainers. He was going for a run after work. Mr. Debois noticed that Albert wasn't behind the counter, and he went downstairs to look for him. Mr. Debois asked his apprentice what he was doing. He saw the baguette and was very cross. He chased Albert around the store room slamming stuff down and going red in the face. Albert escaped, but left his locker door slightly open.

"What do you think you are doing? We only make crusty round loaves!" He pulled the baguette from the locker and the baguette ran away in the running shoes and vest, much to the amazement of the baker and the assistant. "You can't catch me!" he shouted. They ran after him.

He ran down the Champs Elysees where people stared at him and he ran into an old couple who nearly fell over. The old man waved his walking stick at him and the old woman began to chase after the baguette followed by the old man.

"You can't catch me. I have run away from a baker and his assistant and I can run away from you." And he did. Soon he came to the Notre Dame Cathedral and a priest saw him and shouted at him, but the baguette kept on running. "I have run away from a little old couple, a baker and his assistant, and I can run away from you too."

Soon he got to a river and he didn't know how to cross but a dog offered to take him safely to the other side. The baguette saw the priest, the old couple, the baker and his assistant all chasing him so he eagerly accepted and turned, waving to them. The dog licked his lips and his tummy rumbled with hunger.

The baguette was worried he would be eaten when they reached the other bank of the river, so he ran away from the dog shouting "I have run away from a priest, an old couple, a baker and his assistant and I can run away from you."

The dog began to bark and nearly caught up but there was a sudden whoosh of air and the baguette was suddenly flying through the air. He wondered what was happening when he found himself tucked into a guy's shirt. He did not realise he had joined the most prestigious cycle race in the whole of Paris.

The dog, the Priest, the old couple, the baker and his assistant could only watch as the baguette went on to win the race.

MY UNKNOWN HERO BY TINA WATKIN

He watches often from the attic wall with vacant eyes to catch my tearful gaze. Each time I wearily climb the steps I wonder where his feet have wandered in the past.

So young he seems; no down upon his unblemished skin is shown. No marks of battles fought at any stage.

A uniform to show he took the King's shilling, perhaps he lied about his age to join. Just buttons to adorn the jacket. No rank acquired, perhaps this was his first affray.

Would he have had a family awaiting any news, but dreading that sharp knock upon their open door. A mother knitting socks on needles four to stop the chilblains from the evil cold.

A younger sister stitching his initial in blue onto a cotton handkerchief to send when his next birthday should arrive. His father tapping out an empty pipe, no money to refill its bowl, whilst reading last weeks paper and pondering will this war ever end.

Before the soldier left a photograph was taken, enlarged and framed and possibly hung in pride of place above the fireplace. But sadly as the years unfolded, and family died their house and home in ruins lay. No one to salvage precious trinkets once so loved. The picture passed on to his local ale house hanging with others remembered for services given.

But sadly that inn closed, awaiting demolition and everything piled into a brimming full skip.

I stopped my car to check an engine noise and noticed looking out at me from its glassless frame, a beer stained face. I could not steer away and leave him stranded, but stopped and said a silent prayer for him. I quickly turned, yet could not bear to leave him weathering there in elements of disrespect, so gently pulled him from the thoughtless rubble.

Let his last journey be in style, I thought. Carefully strapped into the seat beside me he travelled to his last safe resting place.

The stains still cloud the background where he rests in a simple lightweight wooden frame. I do not know his age, rank or serial number. I've no idea from where he came or his nationality, but I respect that he could have given his life to make my world a better place and honour him, when others passed him by without a care.

He could have been my father, brother, lover or friend if I had been a different age. So I smile at him and sometimes I could swear I see it in his eyes that he is grateful that I brought him home with me.

Who knows, we may one day meet for me to make his acquaintance. I bless the day I found him before the skip was collected and it was not too late for me to save him from a landfill fate. It's comforting to know this unknown soldier might be watching over me now.

A CHRISTMAS CRACKER BY GRAHAM LOCKWOOD

Don Antonio led the party into his magnificent dining room which had been meticulously prepared by his staff. They knew that the Christmas Lunch was one of the most important events in Don Antonio's year and he was not very forgiving if things were not as he had specified. At least the penalty would just be monetary unlike his deceased father who would make any punishments more permanent.

Don Antonio scanned the table, and the arrangement in the room, and nodded at his housekeeper that everything was as he had specified. With a smile of relief, she bowed to Don Antonio, nodded to the staff who silently left. The remaining security guards also left shutting the double doors behind them. They would be stationed outside the door and around the outside of the building but not in front on the windows.

The Christmas Lunch was for his close family and influential individuals who were on the payroll of his criminal organisation. The meal was taking place in Don Antonio's secluded house, set on a promontory surrounded on three sides by the Atlantic Ocean. There was only one road onto the promontory which was carefully guarded and patrolled so any other approaches would have to be over the ocean which would be spotted miles away.

The guests would have preferred to have missed the meal, but if Don Antonio gave you an invitation you would move heaven and earth to be there. It didn't do to offend him, and anyway he was very generous to his guests with jewellery for the ladies and expensive gifts for the men. Both male guests wore the Richard Mille watch that Don Antonio had given them last Christmas. Don Antonio's sources had informed him that within twenty-four hours of last year's meal they had both had the watches and their wife's jewellery valued. He also knew that if anything happened to him these gifts, and any more he gave them today would be sold in a heartbeat.

The room was dominated by the table which was made of mahogany from one of Don Antonio's estates. The cutlery came from Germany, the glassware from Paris and the bone china from England. On the matching furniture around the walls were a few photos of his family. On the far wall, opposite the end containing the log fire was the painting by Manet of the 'Execution of Maximilian' which was completed in 1869. It had taken many years and a lot of money for the original to be replaced by a fine copy and returned to Mexico even if hardly anyone knew it was here. As a Mexican Don Antonio had always admired the image of the European aristocrat who had been imposed on Mexico, being executed by Mexican soldiers.

Don Antonio went to stand behind his chair at the head of the table in front of the painting and once everyone had found their place, he bid them sit, and he followed shortly after. There were just four guests and four members of his close family seated around the table.

On his right sat the Governor of the local state in which most of his operations were based. Don Antonio had contributed to his re-election funding for many years and had also helped with sorting out his previous two marriages. The Governor's third wife was seated on Don Antonio's left, opposite her husband. She was twenty-five years younger than her husband but looked even younger. She had arrived wearing a jacket that matched her fitted dress but had removed it before entering the dining room claiming she was too warm. Her dress was sheer, and she had obviously followed the new trend of not wearing underwear in order to be noticed.

He glanced at her husband who was white as a sheet one second and then flushed the next. Don Antonio could also smell a pheromone scent that was supposed to make her irresistible but not today he thought. Not today.

Don Antonio looked up to see the huge grin that his wife wore, she winked, and her eyes sparkled as usual. He had been married to her for twenty-five years and had not regretted one minute of it. She knew of his business and did not take an active part but managed the family's affairs with a rod of iron. Unlike most of his contemporaries and his father and grandfather before him, he did not have mistresses even though he had received many offers and he suspected the lady on his left would be a willing participant. Don Antonio had been unfaithful to his wife on three occasions and each one was for the sake of his business. After each time he told his wife and made penance at the local church.

On his wife's right side was the local police chief, resplendent in his dress uniform although Don Antonio had no idea where all the medal ribbons had come from. He was an extremely ambitious policeman without any principles at all. He took money from Don Antonio so that he could maintain his various mistresses and cover up his interest in 'Gringo' hippy girls that his men picked up for drug offences. Opposite him sat his wife. She had given him several children but had started putting on weight recently. Her family were extraordinarily rich with interests in politics and oil and the marriage had created a symbiotic relationship. The family received protection from the law and the policeman was promoted way above his abilities or experience.

The middle two places were taken by his two sons. Jaime, the younger of the two was an academic who would go to the best universities if his father's money had anything to do with it. The boy himself was looking forward to the dinner being finished as he didn't like his father's friends and amongst other things, he had been given a new computer for Christmas.

Carlos, his older brother sat opposite was completely different. He was ambitious. As he looked around the table all he could think about was that all this would be his one day, and that day would be a lot sooner that his father realised. In the meantime, he looked at the politician's wife and noticed her making eyes at his father and instinctively knew that his father would not take advantage of her. Carlos decided that he was going to have her one way or another before she left and there was nothing anyone would be able to do about it.

Don Antonio picked up a knife and struck his wine glass and everyone's face turned to him. He lowered the knife, his hands and his eyes and recited the grace, offering thanks for their health and the food that they would soon be eating. Once he had finished, he clapped his hands, the signal for the staff to enter and start serving the meal.

Don Antonio unfolded his napkin and carefully placed it on his lap and then in a family tradition he lifted up the ornate cracker on his plate and offered it to his left. As usual, the crackers had been personally designed by

Don Antonio. They were made specially for this meal and contained luxury items carefully selected for each guest.

The lady to his left tentatively took hold of the end of the cracker and pulled gently. She wanted Don Antonio to finish with the majority of the cracker as it might be seen as an affront if she finished with the largest piece. The end just tore, and she found that she was holding a small piece of the outside wrapper. Don Antonio reassured her that all she had to do was grasp the end firmly, and slowly pull.

The lady blushed and Don Antonio heard a stifled snort from her husband. Don Antonio offered her the cracker again and this time she took a firm hold and pulled hard against his grip on the other end.

Inside the cracker things were not as they seemed. The inside lining of the cracker was made of coloured nitro-cellulose as was the curled-up hat. The gifts had been replaced with plastic explosive and the firing strip was made of a form of gun cotton. The striker was actually a powerful detonator which fired once the strip was pulled apart. The bomb exploded in a ball of flame which then detonated all the other crackers held by the guests or laid on the table until the room was filled with a fireball from which no one survived.

The crackers had been carefully designed to look identical to the ones ordered by Don Antonio for his Christmas Lunch and then substituted. They were the only items that he had personally selected and had been delivered the day before. Not wanting to risk Don Antonio's ire, they hadn't been checked for explosives, though any tests would have simply identified the firing strip and all crackers have those.

The only thing missing from the replacement crackers was a joke, or was it?

THE CUPBOARD BY JULIE PRYKE

It was a lonely job that he did. He was a carpenter and locksmith. He usually started work on the inside of a new build after the other workers had completed their tasks – it was safer that way. But he would have enjoyed a bit of camaraderie at times.

At the moment, he was making an enormous cupboard for the library of this grand house. He was using elm wood at the request of the owner. He had already constructed the library shelves and had to admit they looked excellent. The gentleman had been in and inspected them and even left a few huge tomes to go on them.

He sawed the basic shapes, made the initial joints at the back for the interior shelves. He had measured, sawn, and soaked the doors, fitted hinges and the automatic lock, which, again, was requested by the owner. He just had to check that the doors closed properly before he fitted the runners and the shelves inside.

He checked from the outside. They seemed fine. He went inside and closed the doors, again. Perfect!

Oh, Oh! Now he couldn't get out again as he had forgotten about the unusual automatic lock. He was stuck! He thought of several solutions but most involved damaging his hard work as knocking or shouting were of no use in this empty mansion.

With a sigh, he resigned himself to the situation. He would just have to wait until Professor Tolkein called again to inspect the next stage of his work.

A DEAD LOSS BY ROSE JOHNSON

For the attention of Mr. A Deadloss.
Re: Catastrophe of a funeral

Please note the omission of "Dear" before your name which incidentally aptly describes your shambles of a business. A dead loss and wretched would have been a better choice of address.

I had been recovering from the death of my beloved Uncle Jack prior to the funeral but now quite simply I'm recovering from the funeral. I have a long list of complaints which I am going to bring to your attention so take note, and be very grateful that I am not confronting you in person.

The hearse that arrived with Uncle Jack's coffin was antiquated and scruffy with black smoke belching out of the exhaust. It was making resounding banging noises that reminded us of the discharge of a firearm prompting us to duck in anticipation until we realised what it was. We followed its erratic progress in our cars to the church and watched the coffin which was not properly affixed to the plinth bounce around the back of the vehicle.

As if that wasn't bad enough the hearse slowed to a halt on a hill with the driver cheekily asking us if we could give it a push. For the sake of poor Uncle Jack we did so until it had reached the top where it teetered and swayed before gathering momentum down the other side completely out of control. It must have hit speeds of over eighty miles an hour while the incompetent driver tried to stop it before violently hurtling into the church wall with an almighty wallop.

The force of the collision caused the rear door to swing open catapulting the coffin into the air. Horrified we watched it sailing above us before it eventually landed, fortunately may I add, amongst a bush of prickly brambles.

By this time the coffin lid had come loose exposing Uncle Jack in all his glory. He was down to underwear because some lowlife scum had even taken the suit he should have been wearing.

Lid back on, the coffin was then supported by six pall bearers, two of whom were extremely frail, causing the coffin to sway this way and that. One of the them suddenly dropped to his knees clutching his chest and gasping for air.

We then spent the next half hour applying mouth to mouth resuscitation and cardiac massage before watching the poor unfortunate gentleman being ferried away in an ambulance. It would seem to me that you employ anyone, probably very cheaply, and it was plain for all to see that this hapless soul had exceeded the age of retirement by many years.

We followed only five pall bearers carrying an extremely wobbly coffin into the church to the sounds of Cliff Richard's *Congratulations and Celebrations* when it should have been *Marche Funebre* by Chopin.

Instead of being a sad affair this funeral had become a total farce. We cringed when we heard the vicar get all the facts wrong about our Uncle's life and worse, a tongue tied bible reader stuttered over the word "succour" pronouncing it rather like a rude word.

You did have one redeeming factor though. The music on exiting the church was finally Chopin's *Funebre*, although this is normally played at the start.

The journey to the cemetery proved a bumpy ride yet again for poor Uncle Jack as the replacement hearse was not much better than the first. It lurched and jolted all the way and was driven by a complete novice of a driver.

On arrival the coffin appeared more battered than ever and we were thankful that this embarrassing funeral was almost at an end although it did succeed in finishing with a final humiliating flourish. The rope lowering the coffin was badly frayed completely snapping and causing the coffin to nose-dive to the bottom completely upended.

It took the next half an hour trying to right it difficult when the hole had not been made big enough. It was eventually positioned slightly upward and to one side so with fond farewells we bade a somewhat crooked Uncle Jack a final send off.

By this time I was in floods of tears having been through half a dozen packs of disposable hankies.

We all left the cemetery disgusted vowing to take your bungling company to court and as you can see from this letter the above complaints are manifold.

We will be seeking a very large amount of compensation with additional costs to pay for solicitors, court fees and other expenses incurred.

You will be hearing from my lawyer shortly.

Be warned!

YOURS WITH DISGUST

TOILET TRAINING BY SHEILA GARDNER

Alice and Peter were new to the parenting game. Their son, Alex was a sturdy little boy, full of mischief and had an amazing sense of fun.

Alice had managed breast feeding without too much trouble. Teething was a bit more difficult, sleepless nights, raging fevers and constant dribbling. Now Alice was about to embark on potty training.

Her mother had said that "it was about time". Alice decided to engage the help of Peter. They both agreed that patience and understanding were the key to success.

They bought a charming little potty covered in stars and moons. Alex eyed it curiously, but as soon as Alice and Peter tried to get him to use the potty, he would shake his head and push the potty away.

They were at their wits end. Everyone said that potty training was easy, but failed to divulge their knowledge of this apparently simple task!

Then Alice had an idea. She decided to make up a story about a Potty Pixie, a tiny creature who lived in the potty and sprinkled stardust to make children grow big and strong.

Alex listened, sucked his thumb and tilted his head as he listened to the enchanting tale. He went to the potty and looked into it to see if he could see the potty pixie. He couldn't

Alice said that he needed to sit on the potty and do a little tinkle before the pixie would come.

Intrigued he did as he was told. He sat on the potty and said 'tinkle, tinkle' then looked to see if the pixie was there, but he wasn't.

His mum had to explain what she had meant by 'tinkle'.

At first Alex didn't understand at all.

Alice had another brain wave. She poured water into the potty, saying 'tinkle' as she did this.

Alex smiled and copied her, then when Alex wet his nappy, she pointed to it and said 'tinkle'.

It took quite a while before Alex could grasp the idea that having a 'wee' meant having a 'tinkle' and that having a 'tinkle would make the pixie appear.

Alice had bought a squeaky toy that looked a bit like a pixie, and she would squeak this every time Alex sat on his potty. He began to realise that if he 'wee'd' then the pixie would come.

There was no magic involved just a simple trick to help a little boy to be potty trained!

THOU SHALT NOT BY ASHE BARKER

*Thou shalt not kill, but need'st not strive
 Officiously to keep alive...*

IT WOULD BE A MERCY, really. When you thought properly about it.

It's no life. It's what she would have wanted...

He recited the platitudes in his head, justifying his decision, then he set his cup aside and trudged back upstairs.

She lay where he left her, motionless, her chest barely moving, each breath more laboured than the last. The doctor had only just left. It wouldn't be long now.

"This is no way to go," she'd whispered, her voice barely audible above the rattle in her chest. "Rotting away from the inside. You wouldn't let a dog die like this. You could help me…"

It was a big ask. A massive ask. He'd never done anything like this, never even considered… But there was something in her eyes.

The pillow was in his hands, then it was over her face. She didn't even struggle.

It took longer than he'd expected, or maybe he imagined that. But at last, it was done. She was at peace. No more pain.

He stood back, replaced the pillow where he'd found it. She looked… happy.

Back downstairs he picked up his bag, checked the contents and let himself out of the back door.

It was odd, really, how things sometimes turned out. He'd been passing and spotted the open kitchen window. He only popped in for a spot of honest burglary, never expected to find the old lady upstairs, and certainly never meant to get involved.

But, she'd asked him so nicely to put an end to it all, and it seemed rude not to. Especially as he was making off with her life savings...

FAST TRAVEL BY MATTHEW HOLGATE

If I had a map of the world or maybe a globe, I could imagine myself being magicked into different kinds of adventures. I would lay the map on the floor and shout "Africa/ Safari!"

I would take a deep breath, and whoosh I'm already there, sitting in a jeep where I see a pride of lions roaring at me. Scary some people might say, but I am too fascinated to be scared.

In the trees sit brightly coloured birds like Zazu. I reach for my phone and just as I am ready to take a photograph, a mother giraffe and her calf reach into the tall trees to eat their leaves.

We drive on until we reach the water hole where we see a group of warthogs like Pumbaa. "I hope no one calls him pig", I whisper to my guide.

There's something to see everywhere I look.

Now there is a group of cute little meerkats standing watching me. They are so sweet. I want to take one home, but they are meant to live in a commune, and I would not want to separate them. If they suspect what I am thinking it is no wonder they are checking me out.

After a while it is time to return or visit somewhere else. I have had a thoroughly lovely time.

I close my eyes and shout "Australia/ Sydney!"

There's a list of places I would like to visit including China and Japan and Iceland and the Amazon rainforest.

Travelling like this is ideal because I don't need a ticket or a passport and of course the best part is that it won't cost me a single penny.

It's such a shame I can't take a guest with me!

JUST DESSERTS BY KATHRYN M. HOLGATE

A man goes into a baker's shop. He looks at all the goodies on display in the glass cabinet. After a few seconds he looks up at the assistant.

> Man I would like a jacket potato with tuna please.

Assistant I'm sorry, but we only serve desserts.

> Man Ok, I'll have a hot beef sandwich with red onion and horseradish sauce.

Assistant I am sorry. We only serve desserts.

> Man Right. Hmmm. Can I get pork pie with peas and gravy and mint sauce?

Assistant (patiently) I'm sorry we only serve desserts. (Quickly she adds) The clue is in the name. Just Desserts.

> Man Oh! (He stares at her)

Assistant We have :- Lemon meringue pie, curd tart, cream pasty, jam donuts, currant slice, vanilla slice, bavarian slice, chocolate brownie, chocolate muffins, blueberry muffin, apple pie, cherry pie, gingerbread men, fresh cream chocolate eclairs…

(SHE WAVES HER HAND ABOVE THE GLASS CABINET TO DRAW HIS ATTENTION TO THE CAKES, AND WAITS FOR HIM TO MAKE HIS CHOICE.)

Man I see. (He stands and looks at the cakes.) I'll take a spinach quiche.

Assistant NO! (Big sigh) Only sell desserts!

MR GREY BY JULIE PRYKE

Mr Grey was very sad about his name. He had been ridiculed at school and was still subject to regular abuse, from people who knew him and from others who had never met him before.

The latest thing which had upset him was the comment by the by receptionist at the hotel where he was staying for the conference. "Grey by name and grey by nature, eh? Not like some of the guests we have here!" Mr Grey was scandalised! How dare she talk to him like that?

He'd pointed out to them all that his money was as good as anyone else's. The 'Grey Pound' was very popular these days. All those who were teens in the swinging 60s were now retiring and were perhaps the last generation to have real spending power.

He was retiring soon and looking forward to developing his new hobby. Towards the end of the conference there was a presentation to him from all the staff team and he was delighted to receive the "Superior Magic Set" he had asked for. Not a children's set but a bulky item which he had seen advertised in his favourite magic magazine.

He promised to demonstrate the tricks on the last evening and roped in the receptionist he had encountered before.

"Ladies and Gentlemen, I have two tricks to show you. Firstly, the 'Saw the woman in half' trick which this young woman has kindly offered to assist with...

And secondly" (he said this after he had sawn her in half and everyone was still in shock from the blood leaking out of the box)... "And secondly, the world's greatest trick, 'The Disappearing Man'!" He stepped into the other box, pulled the curtains, and whoosh! A coloured smoke and a drum roll amused them for a while.

Then someone realised that the first trick had been genuine and that the blood was not just stage blood! The curtain was thrust back but all that remained was a message written on the back wall "Thank you, my friends, for my magnificent present; I shall not be seeing you again and shall not regret a minute of your absence!"

It was signed "Graham Grey, the Greatest, Most Colourful Magician that never was!"

FROZEN ASSET BY SHEILA KENDALL

Alf Jones didn't like shopping. Truth to tell he didn't just dislike it he positively loathed it. If he could have gone on his own it wouldn't have been so bad. He could whip round a supermarket in half an hour. He knew that for a fact because he'd done it when Alice was in hospital for her operation.

But the supermarket trip was the highlight of Alice's week and it had to be relished. Alf couldn't understand it. It wasn't as though she enjoyed going. You couldn't call it enjoyment, bullying the other shoppers into submission with your trolley, could you? Accusing the staff of being too slow or too rushed, depending on how she was feeling by the time she reached the checkout. It was totally beyond his ken.

The weekly ritual always began on a Thursday evening. As soon as the table was cleared after tea Alice would vanish into the kitchen armed with notepad and pencil. Eventually she'd re-emerge and get the calculator out of the sideboard drawer. There followed much button punching and muttering about machines large and small being invented purely to confuse her before she returned to the kitchen to knock a few items off the list.

And then came the third, and worst, stage of the ritual. She'd sit in her chair by the fire and begin a long diatribe about his eating habits. Alf knew it backwards by now. He ate too much - she'd had to buy two tubs of margarine last week. He must have spilt half the cornflakes, they couldn't possibly have eaten a full packet in a week.

Alf would sigh and rattle his newspaper a few times although never quite enough to catch her attention. It wouldn't do to attract even more trouble toward his balding pate.

On Friday mornings Alice was up and dressed by eight-thirty. Every other day, Alf was first up and he'd always take her a cup of tea up but that gesture had never once been reciprocated on a Friday. Instead Alice would stomp into the bedroom in her tweed coat and fur hat, her nice, sensible brogues tied in double knots so they couldn't hamper her progress round the supermarket. She'd urge him to hurry as she painted a red slash of lipstick across her thin mouth, making Alf wonder if she was actually in training for a starring role as the Bride Of Frankenstein.

By nine-thirty she'd be sitting beside him in the car, the tightness of her face echoed by the tightness of the seatbelt cinched around her bony frame. Once through the automatic doors of the supermarket she always headed straight for the fruit and veg, a particularly trying area for Alf, full as it was of dark memories.

Not for Alice a pre-packed bag of potatoes. Every single one had to be inspected and weighed before it could pass muster. Once he'd dared to suggest they have a few grapes and he'd almost died of mortification when she decimated the bunch before the remainder met with her approval. It was the one and only time he'd been thrown out of a supermarket.

The soup section was only slightly less horrendous than the fruit and veg. To Alf, one can of soup was just the same as another but not to Alice. The slightest dent didn't escape her eagle eye. It could take her anything up to ten minutes to choose one can of tomato soup. Alf didn't like tomato soup.

It was the same all around the supermarket until they arrived at the freezer section. Alice had to peer in every one of those chest freezers. She poked and prodded the poultry, sniffed disdainfully at the frozen veg and snorted inelegantly over the gateaux and ice cream. Alf wasn't paying a great deal of attention by the time they arrived at the last freezer in the line. Up onto her toes went Alice as she peered into the depths.

"There's only a packet of sausages in here," she informed him.

Alice being Alice, she just had to get near enough to poke at the packet whether she actually wanted the sausages or not. She leaned in a little further and, before Alf's astonished eyes, vanished into the depths.

Alf wasn't normally given to quick thinking. Years of living with Alice had taught him to think long and hard before making any decisions, but Alice wasn't here now. She was in that freezer.

On this particular morning, a whole new glorious vista opened up before his mind's eye. With an agility of foot that would have been the envy of a man half his age, he slammed the lid of the freezer shut and headed for the checkouts and freedom.

Life for Alf settled into a peaceful pattern after Alice's funeral. They'd had a bit of trouble fitting her into the coffin of course, apparently the undertakers had had to thaw her out a bit first. But apart from that the event had gone without a hitch.

There weren't many people present, Alice hadn't been the type of woman to have many friends and those she did have all seemed to drift away from her after her operation. Alf often wondered if she'd actually driven them away with the detailed descriptions she delivered over the tea and biscuits.

Of course there'd been a bit of hassle over the circumstances of her demise. The police found it all highly suspicious at first, but as luck would have it, the supermarket CCTV system had been faulty that day. And, well, an elderly man like Alf wouldn't harm his wife would he? And there was nobody else in the frame, so to speak.

Twelve months passed. Twelve blissfully peaceful months.

Alf took up fishing again, enjoying days on end without having to hear a female voice. He was relieved to be able to whip round the supermarket in less than an hour, enjoying his solitary Thursday evenings by the fireside. His *quiet* Thursday evenings.

Consequently, with all that happiness, the arrival of the telegram came as a terrible shock to Alf.

He'd never known that Alice had a twin sister. A twin sister, moreover, who'd decided to spend her retirement years with them, in the bosom of her family.

In a state of near panic he considered leaving the country, but his passport had expired five years ago and he supposed he'd be too old for the foreign legion now.

And then reason reasserted itself. Sisters weren't often alike. Even twin sisters could be totally different. Nevertheless when the doorbell rang on the Monday morning he answered its summons as slowly as possible in the vague hope that she may go away before he got there. As he pulled the door open the smile of greeting he'd carefully rehearsed before the bathroom mirror slipped from his face.

She stood before him, tweed coat buttoned up to the neck, black fur hat firmly in place. Alf forced his gaze down to her feet as his worst nightmares became reality again. She wore nice sensible brogues tied in double knots, for safety of course.

A VIEW TO A FAIRYTALE BY KATHRYN M. HOLGATE

Emma: Rob my feet hurt. I think I might have a stone in my shoe. Let's stop.

Rob: Okay we can sit on the rock, and admire the view. We are high enough to see right across the valley.

Emma: Nice breeze to cool my feet.

Rob: You're such a wuss!

Emma: Oh, shut up.

Rob: Rude! It's so quiet up here, hardly anyone bothers to come. It's pretty much forgotten. I used to love climbing up this hill, I could leave everyone and everything behind. See over there just beyond those trees, there used to be a castle.

Emma: You mean like King Arthur's or something?

Rob: Yes, but he wasn't from around this area.

Emma: So whose castle was it?

Rob: A minor lord who lost his land, and his head when he betrayed his king.

Emma: I can't see any sign of a castle

Denholme Scribes Scribbling Again

Rob: See where the trees are growing almost in a circle? That was where the tower used to be. The trees are masking it. Some of it is still standing, but not much really. It was only a small and unimportant castle.

Emma: How do you know all this?

Rob: I based some of my dissertation around here. I worked on the site and camped nearby. We used Geo-Physics to map the area, but there wasn't enough evidence to maintain it, so at the end of summer we had to shut down and hand in our findings.

Emma: Oooh! What did you find?

Rob: Nothing of any value. A metal bracelet with birds on, a few bits of pottery and that's about it. Oh, and an old, empty Coca-Cola can.

Emma: That's a shame.

Rob: Yes well anyway I got my degree.

Emma: That seems such a long time ago now. Perhaps if you had found something of value, you wouldn't have finished your course, then we would never have met at Uni.

Rob: Now that would have been a real shame!

Emma: Hey! Listen you…

Rob: You know I'm only joking. I did look into local legends and myths though.

Emma: Did you find anything interesting?

Rob: Yes actually I did. Apparently there was a girl locked up in that tower we were talking about.

Emma: Okay.

Rob: She was a princess.

Emma: Obviously.

Rob: No, I am not kidding love. There was a real princess locked up in the tower called Princess Marie. She was locked away by her father because she refused to marry the man he had chosen for her.

Emma: Good for her!

Rob: Maybe not so good for her.

Emma: What do you mean? Do you think a woman should marry just because a man says so?

Rob: No.

Emma: How did she get out anyway? Did word spread far and wide until one day a handsome prince on a splendid white horse rescued her?

Rob: I wish I could say yes but that's not the end of the story I was told.

Emma: So what happened then? Did her old man die before she got out?

Rob: No.

Emma: The trees grew so thick, the prince couldn't get through them?

Rob: No.

Emma: What then?

Rob: Well, you see she had been up there for so long, they had lost the key to the door of the tower.

Emma: What?! You are kidding!

Rob: No. There was a big battle, and afterwards no-one could find the key.

Emma: You are such a tease Rob Taylor! Now tell me what really happened.

Rob: It's true! No-one could find the key, so they couldn't get into the room.

Emma: How did they get food into the room for her?

Rob: They didn't...

Denholme Scribes Scribbling Again

Emma: What?! She starved to death?! Is that what you are telling me?

Rob: I am afraid so.

Emma: That's ridiculous! They must have got food up to her by a window!

Rob: I don't know if the tower had a window.

Emma: In fairy tales the princess always throws her hair down for the prince to climb up and rescue her. Why didn't she do like Rapunzal and grow her hair long so that she could escape? She didn't need to die. Not like that! Starved to death. It's ridiculous and unbelievable!

Rob: It's not a fairy tale Emma.

Emma: But you would think that someone could climb up the outside of the tower with a rope or a ladder though. Jeez!

Rob: I don't know. I wasn't there.

Emma: Poor girl! Rob, that's an awful story. They could have broken down the door with a battering ram to get her out.

Rob: Maybe they didn't want to.

Emma: Pardon?

Rob: Well maybe they did.

Emma: Can we find out? You could Google it?

Rob: Sorry I can't get any service on my phone. You try.

Emma: No, me neither. Look you told me about this story, so you must know. You are just spinning me a yarn aren't you? It's not a real story at all, is it?

Rob: Sorry to tell you that I learned Princess Marie wasn't rescued by a handsome prince, her father, servant or anyone else. Which means... I suppose that's why it became known as the Black Tower. It is said to be haunted."

Emma: By the princess you mean?

31

Rob: A female ghost has been sighted many times. They say she wears a costume like in medieval times.

Emma: That's so sad. I wish we hadn't come.

Rob: I didn't mean to spoil things for you. Look I'll tell you what I remember: Apparently she was very beautiful. Her hair was as black and as sleek as a raven's wing whilst her skin was the colour of milk, and as soft as a peach. The day she was locked away her mother died, they said it was from a broken heart.

Emma: That's an awful thing to happen.

Rob: Sorry love, that's the legend I was told. If we are to look around we need to get a move on. Are you ready to put your boots back on?

Emma: Yes. The castle is so overgrown, are you sure there'll be anything to see?

Rob: Well you can see where the moat used to be, and the old stone archway is interesting. I'd like you to see that because it's where I did a lot of my research for my dissertation, and we did agree…

Emma: Yeah, I know.

Rob: Obviously we can't climb or get into the tower it's been blocked off, but we can get close enough to see inside it. We'll need to fight our way through the bushes and stuff then you'll see the tower wall. Did I tell you it was called the 'Black Tower' on account of her colouring being so dark?

Emma: No Rob you did not. Is that the only reason for its name? I might as well hear the whole story.

Rob: Well, it's said that she could talk to the birds and they would carry messages to her lover and back.

Emma: That might be the real reason she wouldn't marry the other man. Who was her true love?

Rob: A local lad. When her father found out he had the boy killed and threatened the same for anyone who tried to help her escape.

Denholme Scribes Scribbling Again

Emma: He sounds awful, I hope he died a horrible death!

Rob: As a matter of fact he did. He died from the 'bloody flux', which was a bit like dysentery. There was no cure for that then.

Emma: Serves him right. Anything else?

Rob: It's on Google, Emma. I'll prove it when we get back to the hotel. The birds used to gather in the trees, she used to watch them and called them her friends. It's said that she could talk to them, and she even taught one to speak.

Emma: Very clever. What birds were they?"

Rob: Ravens mostly, but also magpies and jackdaws. They are all intelligent birds. She became known as the 'Raven Princess' and had a tame one that lived in a cage in her room.

Emma: A cage within a cage. That's interesting.

Rob: Yes. So is this. Whenever her spirit is close, big, black, birds gather in the trees squawking and make a hell of a noise. They fly together like a squadron of aeroplanes circling above this castle not far from where we are standing.

Emma: You are joking! Why would they do that? You are just making all this up aren't you?

Rob: No! I swear it's true. I researched it for my dissertation. Look the birds are gathering in those trees. They could be overhead in no time at all. I think we should go. They say that she appears at dusk.

Emma: What?

Rob: They say that sometimes you can sense when she's nearby because there is a rustling noise from the bushes, and a slight breeze just like that one whispering through the branches, and look the birds are flying this way. There are dozens of them now.

Emma: O.M.G. The sky! I don't like this. You are really scaring me now.

Rob: What's that noise? Do you hear it?

33

> Emma: I can scarcely hear you over the din the birds are making. What's going on Rob?

> Rob: Jeez! I think she's nearby. Stay close to me. She's there. Look between the tall trees on the right. Can you see her?

> Emma: No! I am trying not to see. I don't want to. Make it stop. Make her go away. I am scared, Rob.

> Rob: It's her! I don't believe it. It's all true! The whole legend.

> Emma: I am so cold.

> Rob: It's okay love. She can't hurt us.

> Emma: But she's looking straight at us!

> Rob: Thought you weren't looking.

> Emma: Shut up Rob!

> Rob: She's going...

> Emma: Good.

> Rob: She's completely gone now.

> Emma: Quick let's get out of here.

> Rob: Don't forget your boots.

> Emma: Damn the boots! I am off.

VIEW FROM THE WINDOW BY MATTHEW HOLGATE

It was a Sunday afternoon and Will was playing for his local amateur football team, Denholme Rangers. His grandad was going to watch him through the window as he usually did when it was raining or too cold to stand outside. He was very proud of his talented grandson who had scored 24 goals already this season. Today Denholme Rangers were playing Albion Rovers F.C. They were the top teams in the non-league football derby.

Grandad watched as the players got ready. They started their warm up routine of bending and stretching. He felt envious of their energy and youth.

The referee tossed a coin and Albion won. Cameron, their captain broke through into the Denholme half. Will immediately tracked back. From the wings Tom and Joe ran to help him, and after a slight scuffle Joe won. Will raced forward to score his first goal of the match. Grandad cheered loudly through the open window.

" Goaaallll!"

Grandad had played for the team many years ago. Will punched the air and gave the thumbs up signal. Grandad clapped and cheered. Albion Rovers shouted and argued, complaining from the centre circle. They were determined Will wouldn't get another goal, but they were wrong. Everyone was so engrossed in the match that no-one noticed the chap in a navy blue tracksuit and matching bobble hat.

Although Albion played well they were not able to catch the Denholme Team. Things got worse for them in the second half when Cameron, their captain was sent off after an aggressive and dangerous tackle. This gave Will a Penalty shot. He now had a hat-trick!

The final score was 3-0. As the teams dispersed noisily, someone shouted, "Will? Can I have a word with you?"

He was a scout interested in Will attending a trial.

He couldn't wait to tell his Grandad and team mates. They rushed to the pub to celebrate.

SUNSHINE BY SHEILA GARDNER

You are my sunshine, my only sunshine ...

Elizabeth sang the song as she stood in her tiny kitchen, washing up the breakfast plates. Wearing yellow gloves, she vigorously scrubbed the plates, patterned with yellow sun flowers.

What a glorious morning it was. Today she was taking her granddaughter to the park. Becky was the best child ever of course! She had chubby little cheeks and such a beguiling smile, she would put her hand in Elizabeth's as she tottered along to the swings.

Elizabeth felt elated when she thought of the child. She remembered when she had been born two years ago. She had been tiny. She remembered how Becky had curled her little hand around her fingers, remembered the petal softness of her skin, her tiny baby pout. From the beginning Elizabeth had been totally smitten with her granddaughter, calling her her 'little ray of sunshine.'

What joy she had brought the family as they watched her grow, take her first tottering steps. Elizabeth swelled with pride the day she had called her 'granny'.

Grandad, who always had been a bit grumpy, probably because of his arthritis, had, at first not held her. Babies and nappies and sick had never been his 'thing'. But as the child grew, she had tentatively tottered over to him, beamed her sunshine smile and held on to his knees.

He looked at her, not with his usual scowl, but with what could only be described as astonishment. He reached out and placed his gnarled old hand on her tiny pink one and gently said 'hello'.

Becky laughed as he picked her up and put her on his knee. That was the start of a change in Albert. Not so grumpy now, he looked forward to seeing Becky, teaching her to count, making toys that he painstakingly carved from wood. A rocking horse with a flowing main, little trains, wooden blocks. It was as if the child had woven a magic spell to capture her grandfather's heart.

Albert came into the kitchen and put his arms around Elizabeth. Together they swayed and sang *You are my sunshine, my only sunshine,* as they awaited the arrival of their precious granddaughter.

WARNING BY SHEILA KENDALL

The house was quiet, filled with that strange quality of peace which encompasses one at the end of the day. On the wall the clock ticked, marking the passage of time before she must prepare the evening meal for when her husband arrived home. The cat washed himself lazily before the fire, a purr rumbling deep in his chest. With a contented sigh she rested her head on the chair back, her gaze focussing on the picture, a particular favourite of hers, which hung above the fireplace.

She may have dozed off, she could never be certain, her mind searched for a logical explanation for she didn't believe in superstitious nonsense of any sort, and yet, as she looked at the picture, a strange and bizarre event began to take shape.

It was a quite innocuous picture really, just a peaceful stretch of river flowing through sparse woodland, dappled sunlight reflecting onto the path at the side of the water. But along that path a figure began to materialise. It walked briskly along and soon it became obvious it was a man, and that he carried a rifle. She couldn't make out his features, they just formed a pale blob below dark hair, and yet his walk was vaguely familiar to her.

She could hear nothing, apart from the sounds already in the room, but presently the man aimed the rifle and fired at a spot to the side of the path.

As quickly as he had appeared so he vanished. But as she stared at the picture, she saw him again, this time shuffling backwards and dragging the body of a woman. He pulled and tugged the body over the rocks and finally, with a supreme effort, pushed it into the river where it floated for a moment before sinking noiselessly below the water.

It was almost a year after this strange 'dream' that she met the man who was to become her lover. She would never have thought of herself as flighty. She was just another housewife, an appendage to her husband's career, released for social occasions then returned to her grindingly dull cage to cook, clean and attend to his needs. Until that one fateful night.

They met at a cocktail party, one of those events where everybody is exceedingly polite to each other and later, in the safety of their own homes, pull each other to bits. She had gone reluctantly. Her husband was away on business and she always felt a little strange going out without him, but her friend had begged her to go along for moral support so, finally, she agreed. Once there she circulated with everybody else, indulged in social chit-chat and, eventually, came face to face with her destiny. Afterwards her lover declared it was fate which sent her there, to which she would inevitably laugh lightly and say that no, it was her friend's car in which she travelled. For after all she didn't believe in fate did she?

Their affair blossomed through the spring, and by the summer she had become careless, occasionally mentioning his name in conversation when she was at home. After all, her husband never really listened to her any more did he?

It was a particularly warm summer's day when her lover took her to the river. It looked vaguely familiar to her, although she couldn't recall why this should be so. They strolled along the path hand in hand, unaware of the figure following them and presently her lover led her to a patch of grass where they lay down together.

Along the path her husband came walking, a rifle in his hands and anger glazing in his eyes. He came upon the lovers suddenly and, as he raised the rifle, she knew in her final moments exactly where she'd seen this place before but now it was too late to believe in fate after all wasn't it?

The cat sat on the rug, his unblinking green gaze fixed on the picture above the fireplace as his master dragged his wife's body to the river...

ART OF WAR BY TINA WATKIN

In the 50's even girls played Cowboys and Indians, but did we understand exactly what we were trying to capture by dressing up in feathered headdresses and sporting gun belts with shiny pistols, often using noisy caps to add to the reality of gunshots?

In the 80's we tried to destroy each others fleet in the game of Battleships. Years had passed until I discovered that a relative I had never known, was on a ship, the HMS Hood, which was sunk by the Germans in WW2. It chilled me to the bone to think that 1,415 men, some barely adult, suffered this fate and here we had been re-enacting it.

When the 90's arrived I watched my teenage son annihilating armies on the TV screen, and was disturbed to hear the angry cries when he had failed to extinguish lives so freely.

The Millennium was on us and his games became more violent and bloodthirsty. The makers even supplying hand held weapons to shoot at the screen.

The art of war? We all play at little acts of war in our lives. Mine is against pests which eat my plants and produce. I have had occasion to let a spider go for a long swim to Esholt. I'm scared stiff of them.

We might even exclaim we are 'on the warpath' but really just mean we are looking for someone to blame.

We joke now about the War of the Roses. My dad was born in Lancashire and my Mum in Yorkshire. He wore the red rose and she wore the white.

In the real world many face danger, hazards and challenges with no easy solution, like turning the page, put the game back in the box or unplug the device.

Often there is no immediate action which can avert conflict. We must live with it. But remember, try not to start it in the first place.

THE FOLLY BY JULIE PRYKE

Wherever she went she had always counted steps. She could be heard muttering "...twenty-two, twenty-three, twenty-four..." and so on. She tried to avoid the 199 steps at Whitby but could never resist counting a short flight of stairs in the style of the characters on Sesame Street "one, two, three, four, five, six, seven, eight, NINE, ten!"

At one time, her family had worried about her. The doctor they had consulted had suggested that she was suffering from a fairly common symptom within the obsessive-compulsive disorder range. Nowadays they would dismiss it on the rare occasions they saw her, "Oh she suffers from Arithmomania you know!" They saw this explanation as an acceptable one which excused them from paying her much attention – she was happy counting away in her own world!

At the pensioners' group she would count all the cutlery and crockery before and after lunch and happily count the raffle tickets and money before the draw was made. When the pensioners' trip to a local folly approached the tower, the rest of the party paused, almost indiscernibly, as they waited for her to begin, and she did.

"One, two, three, four, five, six, seven, eight, nine, ten, eleven, twelve, thirteen..." And then – Oh No! The young boy came running down the steps and banged into her, roughly knocking her off balance as he chanted "1, 2, 3, 4, 5, 6, 7, 8, NINE, 10".

This broke her off her own counting and disturbed her considerably as she hurried after him to explain that there had to be more than 10 steps up the folly! But he didn't care. He laughed at her and ran off.

She went back to the folly and started again, reaching the eventual 94 that took her to the top of this comparatively short one.

Reaching the top she was still upset and complaining but no-one realised how upset she was until she announced "So, Ladies and Gentlemen, this is my final countdown! One, two, three..."

To their horror, in six steps she had reached the edge of the viewing platform, pushed her slim body through the ornamental opening on the stonework and thrust herself out onto the rocky land below.

GROW YOUR OWN BY ASHE BARKER

"Where do you think you're going?"

"Nowhere," he answered, pulling on his second-best shoes.

"You're always wandering off," she complained. "Anyone would think you had another woman…"

"Perish the thought," he muttered, sliding into his coat.

"Tea's at five. Make sure you're back or the dog gets it."

"Of course, dear." He closed the door quickly and made his way down the path, taking care to pick up his spade as he went.

"I hate that flaming allotment," his wife grumbled, watching him from the kitchen window. "It's not as though he ever grows anything useful."

His plot was ten minutes' walk away, close enough to get to easily but far enough to be sure she wouldn't follow. His wife wasn't fond of walking.

He trotted between the various sheds and animal pens until he reached his own little patch of earth. Dorothy was there, in the next plot, pulling up onions.

He liked Dorothy. Always had. You could have a laugh with Dorothy, and he often did.

"Come over for a cuppa later," he called as he passed.

"Aye, I'll do that. She slung another onion into her basket. "I've got a nice bit of lemon cake to share."

His own crop was coming along nicely. He surveyed the swaying plants in his sultry warm greenhouse with pride, doing a quick calculation in his head. He'd get a few hundred pounds for this lot down at the Kings Head. Dorothy's nephew was an enterprising lad and he'd take it off his hands right sharp.

The lad would usually slip him a few grams of the finished product, too, just by way of being neighbourly. Dorothy would always bake that into a nice cake.

Oh yes, he and Dorothy would have a right old laugh, and maybe he'd take a slice or two of lemon cake home, to have after their tea. That would cheer the wife up.

LOCH NESS BY MATTHEW HOLGATE

The Loch Ness monster lives in Loch Ness, or does he/she?
    Whenever anyone travels to Scotland near Inverness, they invariably visit Loch Ness, hoping to catch a glimpse of the monster. It has become a legend. Some people spend a big portion of their lives trying to prove or disprove, but the truth is no one actually knows because this is a sea loch.

I would like to imagine the Loch Ness monster lives a fantastic life at the bottom of the loch with its bagpipes for company and eating shortbread! Doesn't that sound like a lovely image?

MR. MONET THE CAT BY KATHRYN N. HOLGATE

Once there was an artist called Ted who painted lots of pictures but hardly sold any of them. He was very poor, and lived at the top of an old house that had windows in the ceiling so the light was good enough for him to paint. In the summer it was very hot and in winter it was extremely draughty and cold. He didn't have many friends, or furniture, but there were lots of mice, who came to scare him every night. When he went to bed he shut his eyes so that he didn't see them, but he could still hear them scampering about looking for food.

One sunny morning in May, Ted took three of his best paintings to a new gallery in the next town. He really hoped they would like his work and display his paintings for everyone to see, and buy. The gallery liked one, but asked him to make a some changes to the colour, and fetch it back next week. Ted was really happy, and decided to celebrate. He bought fish and chips for his tea. On the way home he saw a scruffy old silver tabby cat sitting on the wall outside his house. Ted stopped to talk to it and the cat rubbed his chin on his hand. He miaowed to say he was hungry, and it tried to follow him inside. Ted was sad, he would like to have a cat, but he couldn't afford one. So the cat stayed outside, and Ted went up to his room. However, he didn't close the outside door properly, and it swung open so the cat followed the smell of the fish, which lead him to the strong smell of mouse.

Denholme Scribes Scribbling Again

Ted had left his door open, and the cat strode through and sat down beside him.

"How did you get in here?" He asked the cat. "Want some fish Puss?" and broke off a generous portion. When they had eaten, the cat jumped onto Ted's knee, it settled down to sleep, and Ted stroked the soft striped fur. The two were very comfortable and enjoyed each others company all evening, but it was time the cat left now that it was dark so he carried it downstairs and it ran straight back to his room. He went to find it and bring it back down, but couldn't find it anywhere. He checked under the bed, in the wardrobe, under the blankets, where could it be? He tried to coax it, but the cat remained stubbornly in its hiding place. He spent a full twenty minutes looking for it and then gave up.

He got ready for bed, watching out for mice, but was pleased he didn't see any. He thought it strange not to hear scampering feet, and fell into a deep and comfortable sleep. During the night he felt a cosiness, a warmth, and a feeling he was not alone. On the bed curled up beside him was the cat, it was fast asleep and purring loudly. Ted felt elated at seeing his new furry friend again. The mice had been too scared to come out during the night, and Ted was relieved.

After breakfast they went for a walk. The cat in the garden and Ted for his newspaper. The cat was waiting to greet him when he returned. As soon as the door was open it ran upstairs and hid from him. Ted began to paint. When he was nearly finished the cat walked across the paint, smearing colour right across the canvas. Ted had no choice but to alter the painting.

"Now leave it alone" he told the cat. Dutifully the cat went to sleep on the bed. "If you are going to stay, you'll need a name, and you must learn not to touch my paintings. Ok?" Ted thought about names whilst he painted another picture. Eventually the cat came to see what he was doing. He stared at the picture for a few minutes before dipping a paw into the green and then into the blue mixing a lovely shade of turquoise which stuck to his fur, before he smeared it across the canvas. Ted shouted, and the cat ran away, but when he looked at the painting again he decided the coloured shape looked good, and he would keep it as part of his painting.

When Ted took the paintings to the gallery, the owner declared them wonderful, and vibrant. He immediately hung one in the window. Ted decided to call the cat Mr Monet, after the famous French artist. After all they have a similar style he thought. By the time he got home his telephone was ringing. It was the gallery ringing to say they had sold the paintings already and would he paint some more please? Ted painted several more with the help of Mr Monet, and the Gallery sold them quickly too. They asked for more, and sold them too. Soon Teds' pictures were in demand and he could charge a lot of money for them. Every time he sold a picture he bought the cat something in return. He never completed a picture without him. Soon they had enough money to move house. As the cat got older, he became less interested in art, but that didn't matter, because Ted now sold every painting for a lot of money. The cat retired and they lived happily together for many years, and were never troubled by mice again.

NOTHING BY ROSE JOHNSON

The old Victorian hall, central to the town centre, was never short of an exhibition or two and this was no exception.

Part of it had a spacious room reserved for such events with the current theme based around contemporary art by aspiring artists who wished to make a name for themselves. The exhibition had already attracted a good number of visitors, more so this time owing to its unusual content.

An elderly gent in a shabby grey raincoat had been mingling with the onlookers perusing with quizzical interest the concoction of displays. In a prominent position was the bronze sculpture of an upside down tree and at the top a labyrinth of roots from which fruits dangled.

The subject was 'In an upside Down World' with an in depth explanation from the artist, Val Porter, displayed below. She had felt compelled to portray a complex and chaotic world as it is now resulting from climatic changes due to its abuse.

The gent gazed at it for a moment intrigued by the way both the roots and branches wove a complex path, one to obtain water, the other to benefit from the process of photosynthesis. But would either of these processes work in this topsy turvy position. Clever, he thought, as he moved on.

The exhibits seemed to be getting more and more bizarre, but thought provoking nonetheless.

There was a white table with a plate of tomato soup in the middle. The plaque next to it challenged viewers to stir the overfilled concoction at speed trying not to spill the contents onto the table surface. The gent noticed the splashes of several failed attempts around the bowl and it seemed an impossible task not to make any messes. The stirrers were then asked to remove the dish and check the pattern the spillage had made. According to the artist, this was the picture he had intended. The bowl was then reinstated and the spillage cleaned up ready for the next participant.

Interesting surmised the gent. I daresay any image can appear in a spillage he told himself, depending on the individual's imagination. He thought that the last one looked rather like a bed of blooming roses with petals wavering in a breeze, others might see it more morbidly, like a sea of blood or similar.

Exhibit number ten was labelled quite simply 'Nothing' and all the gent could see of it was a rather plain rectangular wooden frame with not a jot or iota in it. It certainly lived up to its description, the interior being completely blank. The inscription next to it asked beholders to select a pen on the table beside and draw or sketch something on the paper.

The gent now curiously observed the attempts of a young lady drawing the arched head of a horse. Rather good he told himself, rather good. In fact after the hasty sketch he decided she had remarkable talent. She turned around catching his admiring look pointing to the last line on the inscription. The print was rather small but he could just about make out the words 'Something can be made out of Nothing'

She smiled as she removed the sketch from its frame offering him the pen. He appeared quite taken aback at being asked, but honoured at the same time.

"You're Joe Slater, renowned landscape artist" she said softly. "I feel so privileged at meeting you." She put out her hand.

"If you're the artist" He said. "Then I should be the honoured one. Indeed something can come out of nothing."

MARK AND MARY BY GRAHAM LOCKWOOD

Mark Harris woke suddenly. He thought he heard voices but that must have been the sound of the milkman outside in the street. They often heard him talking on his phone as he walked past to next door.

He could sense that Mary, the love of his life was laid next to him from the slight depression she made in the mattress. Not wanting to wake her, he slid carefully out of bed without turning on the lights and left the room in darkness.

He had a nagging feeling that today was supposed to be different but as he walked out into the garden, he could not pin down the message he was looking for. The garden was looking beautiful this year thanks to Mary. She loved flowers and gardening, and this was her favourite place when she was upset with the world.

He heard a noise. That must be Mary coming awake and making her morning trip to the bathroom. He chuckled to himself, that was more reliable than waiting for Alexa.

As he approached the bedroom, he saw that the light was on and there were other people there and what where they doing to Mary, his Mary. He watched and felt as though his heart was being squeezed and squeezed as the zip on the large grey bag slipped over Mary's face with sound of a large buzzing bee. Somehow, he sensed he would never see that beautiful face again.

The message he was searching for came closer and he knew he was only seconds away from it being revealed if he just tried harder. They took the bag containing his Mary through the hall and out of the front door where a large van waited with its doors open. They carefully slid the bag containing his Mary into the back alongside another slightly larger grey bag and closed the door.

Mark willed them to stop but the van left, and he found himself next to two policemen. Why haven't they stopped the others taking his Mary? He approached and heard "the pills and the note make it fairly certain that this was a suicide pact. The neighbours say they had been married for fifty-five years. No close family and they had recently been told that she didn't have long to live."

Mark remembered now. The doctor gave Mary just weeks to live when they saw her last week. They only had each other and neither wanted to be alone in this world or the next so they had made suitable arrangements and last night they had decided to be together forever.

But where was Mary? He frantically looked about. Where was Mary?

They had been churchgoers and followers all their lives and fervently believed the message all those sermons had repeated that they would be together on the other side.

Where was Mary? She will be frightened without me, he thought. She was nowhere to be seen.

Mark fell to his knees. They had lied, all of them. All those years of praying and listening to boring preachers. All those wasted Sundays and Holidays. They had lied.

Mark raised his head and screamed "Mary" to an empty universe.

TEMPTATIONS BY SHEILA KENDALL

It arrived with the morning mail. Strategically positioned in the exact centre of his desk it caught Martin's eye immediately.

Marked URGENT the familiar handwriting of his bookmaker rocked his early morning equilibrium.

It was further shaken by the arrival of his secretary. Provocative as ever she sauntered into his office clad in a tight black skirt and crisp white blouse which revealed just enough cleavage to send his blood pressure up a good few degrees on his own personal Richter scale. With difficulty Martin attempted to concentrate on his words rather than her more visible attributes.

"The chairman's secretary wants to book the hotel rooms for the annual conference today," she greeted him.

Martin already had a few ideas about that conference not least of which was a healthy desire to take the luscious Linda along with him. His eyes momentarily glazed over as he reflected on the pleasures of Scarborough in January when the weather would be much too cold for a stroll on the beach but hotels had central heating and cozy bars. They would enjoy a nightcap together and—

"So will your wife be going?"

That question immediately shattered his anticipatory dream and brought reality crashing back in.

"My wife?"

"Yes Martin, your wife. Anne isn't it?"

"Oh no," he babbled, "no, Anne won't want to come. No, not at all."

Linda leaned on his desk allowing another inch of cleavage to reveal itself to his mesmerised gaze.

"I suppose you'll be requiring my ... services."

Martin ran a finger around his rapidly tightening collar and gasped an affirmative.

"I'll book us two single rooms then," she replied removing temptation from his line of vision as she straightened and gave him a rueful smile. "Such a pity you're married Martin."

The breeze of her passing wafted his letter an inch nearer to his nose. Gloomily he slit the envelope and grovelled in his desk drawer for his faithful bottle of vallium before he tackled its contents reflecting that he would have a great deal more grovelling to do yet, principally in the general direction of Anne's feet if he wanted her to release her grip on the marital purse strings long enough for him to pay his debt off.

Not for the first time he reflected on the foolish impulse which had led him to marry her. He should have known that, when she suggested a joint bank account, her own money would be remaining firmly in her pocket. She was no fool. She knew her looks alone would never land her a husband. No, he had been the fool for thinking her wealth was coming his way as soon as he signed the register.

He was still reflecting on the injustices in his life when his eye lit on a client's life insurance folder and he suddenly saw a way to get hold of Anne's money, pay off his bookmaker and, hopefully, get his hands on the luscious Linda in his carefully crafted role of the grieving widower needing comfort in his darkest hour.

Martin had long been a devotee of Agatha Christie and could think of no better tool for his nefarious plans than poison. A sortie round the less salubrious back streets of the city eventually revealed a chemist's shop at the end of a gloomy alley, its dust grimed windows guaranteeing anonymity to the client. The ancient proprietor complemented his surroundings to perfection but, nevertheless, Martin's request for cyanide raised the bushy grey eyebrows by another couple of inches.

"And what would you be wanting that for?" he asked.

"Rats," Martin replied blandly.

"You won't be needing much then."

"It's a big rat."

"Can be the size of a donkey you're still not getting much."

Martin deemed it prudent to get his hypodermic elsewhere assuming that this gentleman would be swift to withdraw the cyanide if he thought he intended to inject his rat with it.

At least his final purchase didn't raise any eyebrows. Lots of men bought chocolates for their wives, they just didn't then carefully inject poison into the centres of them before bestowing them upon their better halves.

To give Anne credit she didn't complain about the likely cost of the chocolates when he presented them the following morning. Actually she didn't say very much at all, just gave him a slightly wan smile and laid back against her pillows.

"Thank you dear, I'll try one a little later," she murmured.

"That's the ticket," he replied breezily. "Right, I'll be off then."

With his financial worries soon to be resolved Martin sang along lustily with the radio as he drove to work, stopping off at a bookmakers (not his usual one of course) to place an odds on bet on the three o'clock at Redcar.

His precious valium lay untouched in his desk drawer as the morning passed in an over-indulgence of dictation, allowing him to gaze rapturously at the lovely Linda as her pencil flew across her shorthand pad. He enjoyed a leisurely lunch at a local hostelry composing his features carefully in anticipation of bad news as he strolled back to the office.

"Oh Martin," Linda greeted him, "there's been a telephone call for you, your wife's been rushed into hospital."

His face dropped into suitable lines of dejection, a trembling hand lifted to his forehead.

"Oh God, I've been half expecting this. She's been ill for quite a while," he murmured with a heavy sigh as Linda extended her own hand in sympathy.

"Can I be of any help?"

Never one to pass up an opportunity Martin was swift to take on the role of the helpless male.

"I suppose she'll need some of her things, nighties and soap and - I wonder - would you mind sorting them out for me, I'm hopeless at that sort of thing."

Linda didn't mind the thought of grovelling through Anne's cupboards at all. She was more than willing to visit her rival's home. A house which had her eyebrows rising as Martin turned into the driveway before the sprawling detached residence which, by her swift calculations, his salary alone certainly couldn't pay for. Those same eyebrows dropped abruptly when he offered to show her the bedroom before she was even through the front door.

"Why don't you make us a cup of coffee and I'll find my own way round," she replied firmly.

Slightly disgruntled he withdrew towards the kitchen leaving the lovely Linda to discover Anne's equally lovely fur coat all by herself. It was while she was admiring the effect of that coat upon her perfect proportions that she espied the box of chocolates on the bedside table and selected a coffee cream for her delectation...

The shrill ringing of the telephone startled Martin as he was about to take Linda's coffee upstairs to her. He briefly considered ignoring it but, if Linda had heard it, it might appear suspicious if he did.

"Mr Jackson? St Winifred's Hospital here. Just to let you know your wife is fully recovered and you can collect her any time now."

"Did you say recovered?"

"Yes. There's nothing to worry about, just a fainting spell. Quite common in early pregnancy."

The sudden dull thumping of his heart was echoed by a heavy thud from the upper reaches of the house.

He absentmindedly took a sip of scalding hot coffee a lone chocolate rolled down the stairs to land at his feet.

FOOLS RUSH IN BY SHEILA GARDNER

The ending to the proverb is ...where angels fear to tread.

It's part of a poem by Alexander Pope, entitled "an essay on criticism. The proverb was to show the folly of people who chose to venture into dangerous and unsafe situations. Angels in this proverb represent the wise, mature, sensible individuals who are generally focused and level headed.

So angels can be said to be good, thinking, steady people who consider any situation before taking any action. Some might say boring individuals, fuddy duddies without a sense of adventure who never leap into the unknown without considering the consequences. Given that risk taking is potentially dangerous, why would you?

Maybe the risk takers do it because they enjoy the adrenaline rush, disregarding the fact that there is no sense in it.

But where would we be without these 'fools', these risk takers?

Think of the adventurers who discovered new continents, who sailed into the unknown believing that the world was flat, curious to know the truth. Back they came with exotic fruits and tales of the vastness of the world. What of the pilots who flew the first planes trusting the flimsy constructions, never questioning how on earth they stay up in the sky.

The rush of adrenaline must have been great indeed as they flew into the bright blue yonder amidst fluffy white clouds.

So, were these risk takers fools who intrepidly strode into the unknown regardless of where angels fear to tread?

DENHOLME SCRIBES.

Who are you?
Wise as I am, I am, I think a risk taker. Does that make me a fool?

THE TAX BILL BY ASHE BARKER

It's one of those 0345 numbers. I hit 'reply'.
"Can I speak to Martha Morris?"
"Speaking."
"This is HSBC Fraud Investigation. Can I run through some identity verification?"
Heart sinks. "Okay."
There follows ten minutes of head scratching, educated guessing and frantic looking up. Memorable word, name of maternal grandmother's cat, first school. Eventually satisfied, the disembodied voice continues.
"Do you recall a payment of nine thousand pounds from your account?"
"I do. I made it ten minutes ago."
"So you *do* recall…"
"I just said so."
"What was the purpose of the payment?"
"Tax bill."
"Did someone ask you to make the payment?"
"Yes. Her Majesty's Revenue and Customs. HMRC."
"Were you expecting this request?"
"I was, because I have the tax demand in my hand."
"Is this a regular payment?"
"It's my tax bill!" *(losing patience)*

"Is anyone pressuring you to make this payment?"

"Not yet, but I expect they will."

"So, you *are* being pressured?"

Starting to feel more than a little irritated, "Yes, I mean no."

"Can you answer me, please?"

"It's a tax bill." *Gritted teeth.*

"Are you expecting any further similar requests?"

"Did you say this call is being recorded?"

"Yes, madam. It is."

"Thank God for that! Is there, then, the remotest chance that anyone senior to you with even the most tenuous grasp of British tax law might be listening?"

Awkward silence. The voice rallies, and ploughs on undeterred.

"If these funds are released, the bank may not be able to recall the money if the transaction turns out to be fraudulent."

"I don't want the money recalling. I want you to action the payment so I can pay my f....... tax bill!"

"Is anyone there with you?"

"No."

"Are you in a public place?"

"I'm in my front room."

"What about friends? Family?"

"Let me be clear. I'm alone. It's just me and my tax bill. I confirm I tried to make this payment. I know what I'm doing. It's not a scam. It's just me, doing ordinary things. Please. Pay. Up."

"Madam, I should warn you… Did you see the Fraud Protection advice?"

"I did, but this isn't a fraud."

"Do you remember what the advice said?"

Count to five. Twice. "I do, but…"

"Can you recall it?"

"Not word for word."

"Madam, I need to advise you—"

Reins in temper – barely. "Thank you for your concern, however misplaced. But really, there's no need for you or the bank to worry."

"The payment has been flagged."

"Unflag it."

"Can you recall the exact amount of the payment?"

"Nine thousand pounds."
"And what is the purpose of this payment?"
"Tax bill."
"Why are you—?"
End of tether. Hang up.

HAT TOWN BY MATTHEW HOLGATE

In the busy town of Hat Town everyone wore hats and all the shops sold hats too!

"Hats, hats, hats. Come on, roll up and grab a bargain for yourself. I have hats for every occasion," called the guy in the yellow top hat at the market stall.

"Yes, but they are not as good as mine," shouted a young man in a striped woolly hat.

"Or mine," yelled a woman in a very fancy bonnet trimmed with lace.

I was so surprised to find absolutely everyone except myself had a hat on. What was happening here? Who were these people? I don't remember how I got here. I now understood how Alice felt when she arrived in Wonderland.

Maybe similar to Alice, I am in a dream and perhaps I'll wake up soon. No harm in entering into the spirit of it though. Rather like Wonderland all the trees and flowers wore hats of bright colours. Every post, fence and chimney pot were decorated with hats or shaped like a hat from different countries.

The Mayor of Hat Town wore an especially tall top hat. He saw I wasn't wearing mine. "Hey, you, where's your hat?"

"Sorry," I replied. "I don't have one."

"Yes you do," he replied crossly. I put my hand in my pocket to show him I really didn't, and pulled out a flat, round disc. I was very surprised. I watched it grow larger until it turned into a hat. I thought there might be something inside it, so I reached in, and pulled out a white rabbit. I placed the hat on my head. The rabbit told me his name was Ted. I was now a member of Hat Town.

REFLECTIONS BY SHEILA GARDNER

Who is that person who stares at me, peering through rheumy eyes to get a better look at the ever-present wrinkles? Eyes sunken and sad, she looks tired.

Well, I suppose that's a polite way of saying haggard. Her mouth turns down at the corners making her look even sadder, older? Her hair is a lightened colour, the colour of straw, wispy, shoulder length framing her face. Even when she smiles, that smile does not reach her eyes. The smile merely accentuates the wrinkles.

What lies behind this wrinkled façade? What secrets lie beneath the surface, undulating in the murky depths of her mind? Where did she come from, this woman who looks at me? What journeys has she been on to get here? Did she know the soft touch of a lover, the joy of being alive, walking in a wood carpeted with bluebells, the melodic burbling of a stream? All the beauties and wonders of the word, the sights and sound of a world teeming with colour and smells and noise.

I look into the depth of her eyes. It is said that the eyes are the gateway to the soul. I turn away from the mirror, the image that does not reflect the real me.

I carry the knowledge of a rosy cheeked child who tottered into the world full of wonder and hope. I know that teenager, shy, clumsy, awkward, standing in the shadows watching. Always there but never present, preferring to be "the watcher."

Reflections by Sheila Gardner

I know the traumas of her life, the ribbon of her life, winding and flowing like the river as it makes its way to the sea, sometimes calm, sometimes a raging torrent of wrath and foam. At times serene as the sun dapples its smooth surface, at times wild and untamed swirling eddies of darkness.

I was there when she gave birth to her children. I shared her joy, her passionate desire to protect them.

I was there when she laughed and sang and drank red wine without a care in the world, I was also there to witness the sadness, the sense of not belonging. When life was too raw, I felt her pain. I was there when she overcame obstacles, rising above the feeling of worthlessness to study, so she could make a better life for her children.

I witnessed her inner strength and determination, her thirst for knowledge, her pure joy in her well-earned success. The hardship toughened her. The learning strengthened her. As she grew she gained in confidence, no longer the shy, retiring weed, but like a blossoming flower with its face turned to the sun, she stood tall and faced the world.

COFFIN FLY BY GRAHAM LOCKWOOD

John was a writer. An avid writer rather than a good one. He liked writing novels, short stories, poetry and any type of verse.

He hadn't had any of his compositions published, but that wasn't the reason he spent all his spare time writing.

He carefully organised his time so that he could write without any interruptions. He had found the Covid restrictions an ideal excuse to spend even more time writing. He had a P.C. in his conservatory with the keyboard carefully positioned so that he could write for hours without any distractions or discomfort. And when he discovered Spotify, he had even less reasons to stop writing, as he had bought himself a very expensive pair of wired headphones, so he didn't need to change the C.D.s anymore.

One sunny afternoon he was well into some romantic fiction he was writing when a fly, not as big as a blue bottle but bigger than a gnat, flew slowly in front of the screen and exited John's eyeline to the left. He had just refocused when it came back in an eccentric loopy flight and settled on his keyboard. He waved it away and resumed his typing. Seconds later it was back on another part of the keyboard and again it flew off. To John, it looked like the fly deliberately waited until he resumed before making another zigzag flight onto the keyboard. This time he waited for it to move but when it didn't, he swore out loud and with a grand sweeping gesture encouraged it move on.

John now realised that he was watching the fly rather than concentrating on his work. It was on the window, then the top of his screen, then the table and back to the window and every two or three moves it landed on a key on his keyboard.

Out of curiosity, John took a photo of the fly as he didn't recognise it, although there was no real reason he should. He decided to take a break and made himself a large coffee, most of which went into his vacuum flask for later consumption as there had been too many interruptions already today.

Whilst waiting for the coffee to cool he used his phone to look for an App that would tell him what sort of fly was bothering him. Once he had found one, he sent a copy of the photo together with a request for an identity of the bothersome fly. When he sat back in front of his keyboard the fly was on the top of the screen just above the camera. There was reflected light both from the camera lens and the fly's eyes as it seemed to be carefully considering him.

Just as he raised his hands to start typing, his phone pinged. With a sigh he picked it up and spotted it was a reply to his query about the fly. John looked up and he was sure the fly was waiting for him to finish. It just sat there looking back at him staring.

The message told him that the fly was a Megaselia Scalaris from the family Phoridae and is better known as the scuttle fly (from its lack of flying ability), humpbacked fly and more famously a coffin fly. John sat back puzzled. Where the hell had that fly come from? Now determined to get rid of it, John quicky skimmed through the file and noted that the female coffin fly can burrow down through two metres of wood and soil to lay her eggs, the equivalent of a human digging down two miles. Coffin flies are also picky as they prefer lean meat for their eggs whilst most beetles that consume dead meat prefer fatty tissue. A human body can be consumed by coffin fly larvae in as a little as one year or as long as eighteen depending on the ambient temperature.

Michael shuddered and quickly put down his phone and as soon as the phone touched the table, the fly moved and landed on a key. Reacting quickly John prodded the key but living up to its name the fly scuttled sideways. He missed, then missed again.

By now John was angry. He kept stabbing away until eventually he stabbed hard, and the fly didn't move. He felt it squash under his index finger.

John groaned. He should have just swept it away. Getting a tissue, John slowly prised it off the key, gave the key a wipe and then checked his finger but gave it a wipe anyway just to be sure. Just to emphasise that he was the victor in this contest, John unlocked the back door and ostentatiously holding the tissue at arm's length he walked to the bin, lifted the lid and dropped it in. He returned to his computer, made himself comfortable and checked to see how far he had got with his story. He read:

"We are waiting."

ADAM AND EVE BY JULIE PRYKE

"Well!" said Eve, "that was a surprise. You could have knocked me down with a feather!"

"Where would I get a feather from?" asked the snake, who always took things very literally.

But Eve wasn't listening. She was too upset. "I never expected that to happen, right back from the first day I met him, I never thought he was like that".

"Now, now" said the snake in his most charming, ingratiating manner. "Don't you worry about it, pet, I can help you, I've got the perfect solution and it will never happen again, I promise." He pointed slyly towards the apple tree.

"Why should I take any notice of you, you big slithering lump? When have you ever come up to with any useful suggestions?" Eve grumbled.

"Well only the other day I suggested that if you put that cracked ostrich egg onto a rock, it would fry up nicely, make a nice, unusual meal".

"But then you had to go and spoil it by eating all of it yourself!" she countered.

"Sorry Eve, that was my mistake," he hissed, "but I do love you really!"

"A lot more than that Adam" she agreed. "I mean, another woman! Where did he get her from?"

TEE SHIRT BY SHEILA GARDNER

I have a tee shirt that I bought when I took my children to London for their first visit to the capital. I bought this tee shirt in a place that was encouraging people to emigrate to Australia. My children were fascinated by the objects in the shop. A boomerang, cuddly koala bears, a didgeridoo and pictures painted by aborigines.

I was studying to be a teacher at the time and would look for fascinating and interesting topics for my children to ensure that their education was expansive. The tee shirt caught my eye because it was black and white. The motif on the front was a painted crocodile with white lines to represent water. The style was simplistic and the children loved it too. I still have that tee-shirt, a treasured memory of the special time we had together.

Many years later I went to Jamaica and whilst there I visited the mangroves. Lurking in the murky waters, entangled with the roots were lots of crocodiles. This was my first sighting of a real live crocodile. Not at all as I expected, they were not very large, not as scary as the huge ones that I encountered basking on the banks of the Nile.

I have often wondered what the crocodile symbolises. For instance, the koala bear makes you think of Australia, whereas cats remind me of Egypt. I think that one of my favourite places is India, the vibrancy of its teeming life. Most of all I love the majestic elephants with their swinging trunks and their ability to never forget!

THE WEB BY JULIE PRYKE

Spider lay comfortably in his loosely woven hammock, which he affectionately referred to as his Web. He was deep inside his underground lair, well in his mum's cellar, with a single light shining dimly.

He had set up his mobile phone as the prime controller, his PC, laptop and tablets all sitting in their usual positions, all primed for 'lift off'.

He grinned as he assessed his plan for the final time. He had identified the 470 accounts he was aiming to break, all held by world banks and huge corporations.

He had established many off-shore accounts and was delighted that, having tested them thoroughly, he could see that none of them had any way of linking one to another, no back doors could be found.

Now he set into action, the programme he had been designing and working on for so long.

Watching it as the funds tumbled out of their home and then appeared in one of his many accounts was such a delight. He rejoiced that those with the most capital in the world would all suffer from his actions.

Within seven minutes he was the richest man in the world and left the screens to get the champagne and roast chicken he'd bought and hidden earlier, from his mum..

On his return he was horrified to see that his accounts were emptying as quickly as they had filled up. He worked frantically to prevent it all being lost, but to no avail. How on earth was this happening?

The Web by Julie Pryke

He then realised that there was a back door in his prime controller which had been discovered and was being put to good use. And, based on the message he received at the same time, a bigger spider than him, calling herself, 'The Black Widow' had drawn him into her web and annihilated him.

But he'd be back!

MARTIN'S DREAM BY GRAHAM LOCKWOOD

Martin flashed awake.

At first, he was confused where he had been sleeping but realised that he was back in his own bed at his mother's house. He recognised that mark on the ceiling that no matter how much it was painted over was still visible in the early morning sun. Shards of sunlight came through the gap in the curtains, and he could see the dust motes dancing in the light.

As he threw back the duvet, he watched these particles of dust dance and twirl as the air raced past. It looked like another beautiful day, and he intended to make the most of it. Quickly, he showered and dressed in his favourite jeans, shirt, and trainers.

Martin skipped downstairs and headed for the kitchen. From the lack of noise, he realised that he was on his own in the house so set out to get some cereal for breakfast followed by a large cup of his special coffee. After checking the time, he realised the need to get a move on so grabbed his stuff, locked the door, and headed across town to meet up with Georgia. He had known Georgia for many years, but they had only started dating in the last few weeks and Martin was happy. Very happy.

He started with a steady walk but was so looking forward to seeing her again he found himself putting in an extra skip or two and jogging across the traffic stream instead of waiting for the vehicles to clear. Soon he was approaching the drive to Georgia's parent's house and his heart was pounding in his chest in anticipation of seeing her or of finding that she wasn't at home.

He was nervous as he knocked on the door and counted down the seconds before daring to knock again. As he reached up to knock, the door opened, and she was there. He stammered a greeting but couldn't think of what else to say at that moment. She solved his problem by suggesting they go for a walk up the hill behind the town as it was such a lovely day.

She exited the house, locked the door and they kissed. Everything was all right. She smiled at him, then took his arm and led him off towards the hill about two miles away. As they walked, they talked, and they laughed and were oblivious to everyone else. But everyone else who saw them smiled a little smile.

Once they reached the summit, they found a seat and enjoyed the view, the sun and each other. They laughed and they talked and after an hour Georgia raised a finger and touched it to Martin's lips.

"Shhh" she said. "My parents have gone out for the rest of the day. I want to go back."

They made their return hanging on to each other in almost total silence. Martin was nervous when Georgia opened the door, but she reassured him that they were alone.

They had furious sex on her bed with the curtains wide and the sun beating down on them. Then they made slow, quiet love until they were tired. Martin woke and chased a bead of sweat down the line of Georgia's back and then gently brushed the fine blond hairs on the back of her neck highlighted by the sun's rays.

Once they were completely awake, they showered, made themselves a drink, and then walked down to the river holding tightly on to each other's hand. They stopped at a small café and managed to get a seat outside where they could sit opposite and enjoyed a small meal, a drink of wine and each other. As it was dusk, Martin walked Georgia back to her parent's house. Reluctantly they kissed and parted, and Martin made his slow way home.

Before long he was back in his bedroom and getting into bed. All he could think was that this was the best day in his life, and he wanted to do the same thing tomorrow.

As his eyes closed, he felt a familiar kiss on his forehead. He opened his eyes slowly but there was no-one there, so he dropped off to a contented sleep.

Inches from his forehead, Martin's mother raised her head from the comatose body of her only son. She had never felt so old, and the weight of the next few seconds bore down on her but with help from Martin's sister and father she managed to return to an upright position. If there was such a thing as a 'Death Kiss' she had just given one to her son as he lay on the hospital bed covered in bandages and attached to so many tubes and wires. In the corner were a bank of instruments all giving out a steady whine.

Martin had been in a coma in the hospital ever since a drunk driver had crashed into him and Georgia on their way back from the river several months ago. Georgia had died instantly and had already been buried but Martin had continued to live by some unknown miracle. The medical staff had assured and reassured her that there was no chance of a recovery or any signs of any brain activity.

There was a quiet cough from the doctor and all the family turned to the displays in the hope that at that moment there would be a sign, any sign. They weren't asking for an Everest or a Snowdon but just some small deviation in the flat lines that would prove that Martin was still with them.

Martin's mother nodded and the doctor turned off the life support and all the displays disappeared.

Martin died for the second time in his short life.

ALSO BY DENHOLME SCRIBES

A Collection of Our Scribblings, May 2022
Some Christmas Scribblings, November 2022
Some More of Our Poems, October 2023

ABOUT THE AUTHORS

The Denholme Scribes come together every Tuesday morning to share our latest literary efforts, discuss ideas, and support each other. Coffee and cakes set the stage, and experienced writers and newcomers alike are welcome.

Each member brings their own ideas, genres, and styles. Whether it's evocative poetry, short stories, or personal essays that offer glimpses into lived experiences, the Denholme Scribes embrace the power of storytelling in all its forms.

Every year we publish a collection of our poems and prose. This, our latest collection of short stories, is a celebration of our dedication and hard work throughout the year.

You need look no further if you want a cracking Christmas present for your friends and families.

Enjoy!

Printed in Great Britain
by Amazon